A Merry Fair

by Jodie Shepherd
illustrated by The Artifact Group

Ready-to-Read

SIMON SPOTLIGHT / NICK JR.
New York   London   Toronto   Sydney

Based on the TV series *Nick Jr. The Backyardigans*™ as seen on Nick Jr.®

SIMON SPOTLIGHT
An imprint of Simon & Schuster Children's Publishing Division
1230 Avenue of the Americas, New York, New York 10020

Manufactured in the United States of America
2 4 6 8 10 9 7 5 3
Library of Congress Cataloging-in-Publication Data
Shepherd, Jodie.
A merry fair / by Jodie Shepherd ; illustrated by The Artifact Group. — 1st ed.
p. cm. — (Ready-to-read)
"Based on the tv series Nick Jr. The Backyardigans as seen on Nick Jr."—Copyright p.
ISBN-13: 978-1-4169-4798-1
ISBN-10: 1-4169-4798-1
I. Artifact Group. II. Title.
PZ7.S54373Mer 2008
2007024648

"I am merry!" says .
PABLO

"So I am called Merry ."
PABLO

"I am merry too," says .
TYRONE

"I am Merry ."
TYRONE

"I am also merry," says ,
UNIQUA

"because today is the fair."
CASTLE

"Princess lives at the ,"
TASHA   CASTLE

says Merry .
TYRONE

"She never smiles," says .
PABLO

"We will go to the fair
CASTLE

and make her smile," says .
TYRONE

"Which way to the  ?"
CASTLE

asks   .
TYRONE

"I see nothing but   ."
TREES

"Oh, no!" cries   .
PABLO

"We are lost!

This is not merry at all."

So Merry  climbs on
UNIQUA

Merry 's shoulders.
PABLO

And Merry climbs on
TYRONE

Merry 's shoulders.
UNIQUA

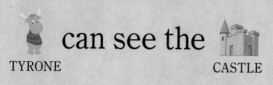 can see the

TYRONE CASTLE

over the tops of the .

TREES

"It is over there!" says  .

TYRONE

They go on their merry way.

"Halt!" a knight calls out.

It is Sir 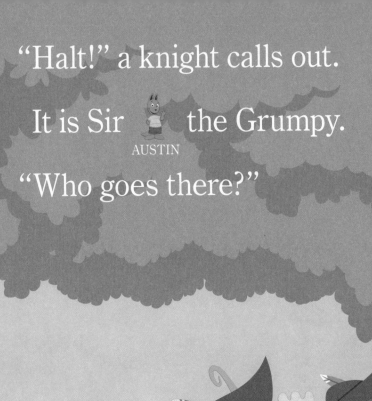 the Grumpy.

AUSTIN

"Who goes there?"

"We are two merry men," says 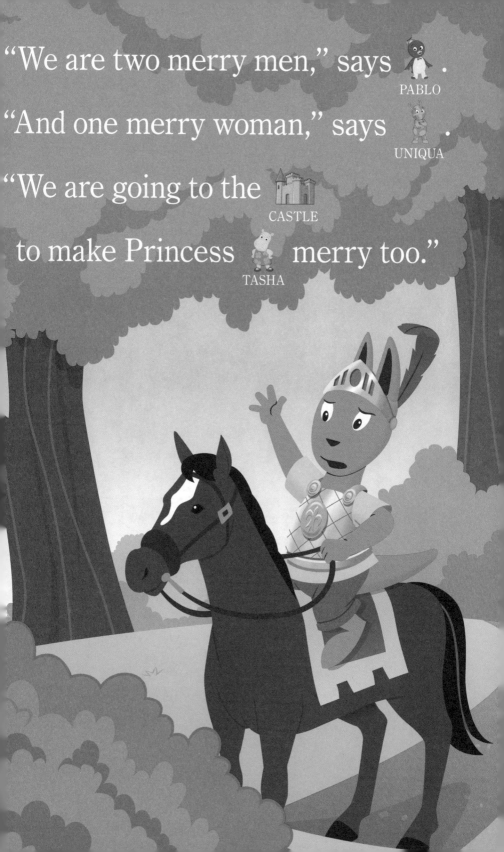 PABLO .

"And one merry woman," says UNIQUA .

"We are going to the CASTLE

to make Princess TASHA merry too."

"Well, I am not merry,"

says Sir  the Grumpy.

AUSTIN

"I am grumpy.

And you may not pass."

UNIQUA plays a merry tune.

PABLO and TYRONE dance a merry jig.

Soon Sir AUSTIN smiles.

"I feel merry now.

Just call me Sir AUSTIN the Merry."

"If we can turn

Sir 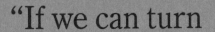 the Grumpy

AUSTIN

into Sir 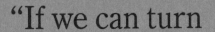 the Merry,

AUSTIN

surely we can make

Princess 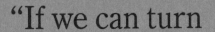 smile," says 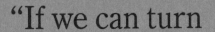 .

TASHA   PABLO

They go on their merry way.

Finally they come to the .
CASTLE

But the fair is not merry at all.

Princess  is alone.

TASHA

She looks very sad.

 dances around.

UNIQUA

 and Sir  leap and

TYRONE   AUSTIN

tumble.

Princess  starts to smile.

TASHA

Look! 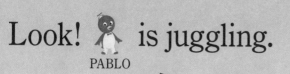 is juggling.

PABLO

He juggles 4 🍅 at a time.

FOUR   TOMATOES

SMASH!

 needs more practice!

PABLO

But Princess looks merry.

TASHA

"The 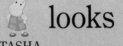 made you smile!"

TOMATOES

says  .

PABLO

"No," answers Princess  .

TASHA

"It was not the  .
TOMATOES

It was all of you!

Having friends at my 🏰 fair
CASTLE

makes me feel very merry."

"We are three merry men," say Merry  ,  , and  .

PABLO   TYRONE   AUSTIN

"And we are two merry

women,"

add Merry  and .
UNIQUA   TASHA

"What a merry adventure!"

says .
TYRONE

"Those made me hungry,"
TOMATOES

says 🐧.
PABLO

"Let's go to my 🏠 for a snack."
HOUSE